THE Misfortunes OF CAPTAIN CADAVEROUS

by Kaye Umansky

Illustrated by

Judy Brown

BBC BOOKS

Published by BBC Books,
a division of BBC Enterprises Ltd,
Woodlands, 80 Wood Lane, London W12 0TT
First published 1992
The moral right of the author has been asserted
© Kaye Umansky
ISBN 0 563 36331 2
Illustrations © Judy Brown
Set in Caslon Roman u/lc by Goodfellow & Egan Ltd, Cambridge
Printed and bound in Belgium by Proost NV
Colour separations by Dot Gradations Ltd, Chelmsford

Captain Cadaverous was walking on the deck
In his very best pyjamas (which were green and yellow check),
When a passing cheeky seagull dropped a present down his neck
Squawking, "Anyone for seconds? I'll be back in just a sec!"

From that very moment onwards, it was downhill all the way.
His breakfast bowl of porridge was a nasty shade of grey
And the cabin boy who brought it, to the Captain's great dismay
Blew his nose upon the serviette and sneezed upon the tray.

His cup of morning coffee when they brought it through to him
Had a crack from top to bottom and three chips around the rim,
But what *really* got him hopping mad, what *really* made him grim
Was the cockroach who was using it to take a morning swim.

The man who came to shave him, poor Cadaverous did note,
Had these very shaky hands and lots of bloodstains down his coat.
"I think I'll grow a beard, you know, just while we are afloat,"
Said the Captain, very firm, before the razor touched his throat.

Then from the deck arose a lot of fierce and threatening cries,
The seamen had collected and were yelling for a rise,
"'Tis mutiny!" the barber said, with wildly rolling eyes.
The Captain merely shrugged; to him, it came as no surprise.

"All right now, boys. The banks are closed, I fear. It's Saturday.
Besides, the nearest cash point is a thousand miles away.
I fear I'm rather short right now. But you'll all get your pay
The moment we weigh anchor at the port of Biffin Bay."

"Oh ar?" replied the seamen, "us 'ave 'eard that one afore.
But us knows that beneath yer 'at you got a secret store.
So give us what be owin' us before us goes ashore
Or you'm askin' fer a mutiny. 'Tis money or 'tis war!"

The seamen were real cutthroats
and they looked and sounded tough,

With names like Mick McMuckypup and Phil O'Fisticuff,

Ben Bones and Tattoo Tony,

Wild Boy Will and Old Dan Druff,

Blind Ken and Dick Delinquent.
Do you think you've heard enough?

It was lucky for the Captain,
Who was in a nasty spot,
That there came an interruption.
Bet you're dying to know what.
A cry came from the crow's nest.
(Are you following the plot?)
And the Look Out hurtled down,
And lay complaining he was shot.

Now the Look Out had a stammer, and his tongue would tend to trip
Over certain words that always seemed to paralyse his lip,
But he did his best, poor fellow, though in death's cold, icy grip,
Mumbling, "P–p–p–p–p–p–p–p–Pirate Sh–sh– Ship!"

Imagine all the panic, all the cries of "Lordy me!"
All the shouting and confusion and the pointing out to sea.
"I take it," sneered Cadaverous, "there's now no mutiny?"
"Oh aye. We'll have it later," said the seamen sheepishly.

"I have a plan," the Captain said, "and here's what it entails.
We Turn Around And Run Away. It very rarely fails.
This craft, the ILL WIND, really shifts; those pirate tubs are snails.
We'll set the sails, and then we'll – by the way, where *are* the sails?"

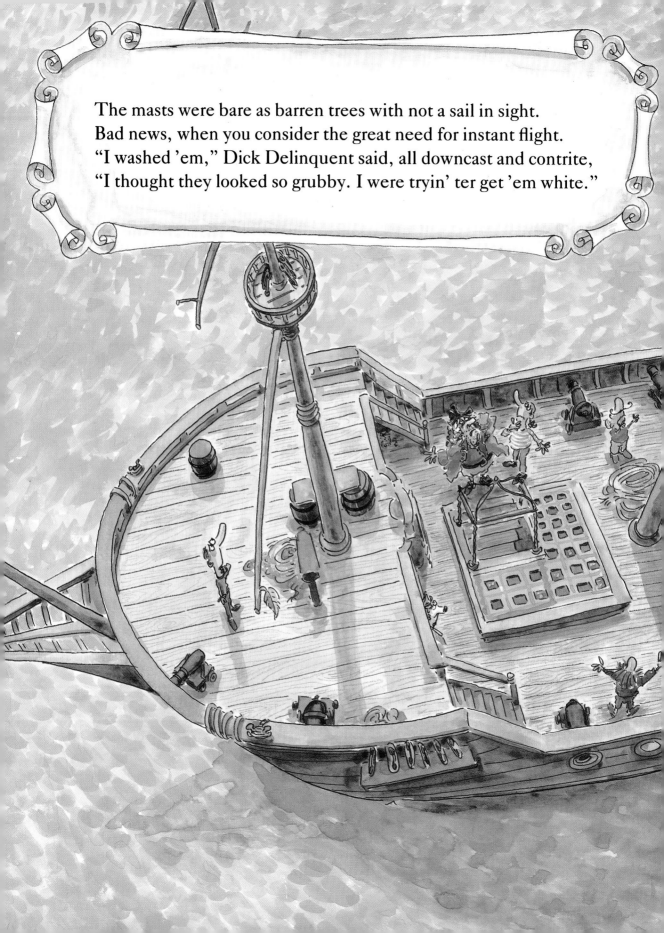

The masts were bare as barren trees with not a sail in sight.
Bad news, when you consider the great need for instant flight.
"I washed 'em," Dick Delinquent said, all downcast and contrite,
"I thought they looked so grubby. I were tryin' ter get 'em white."

And all the while, the pirate ship was ever drawing near
With the Jolly Roger flapping, very grim it did appear.
"We'll have to fight," the Captain said, "the situation's clear.
And by the way, Delinquent, that's the end of your career."

"Now, man the guns, you mariners, or it will be too late."
It was. A sneaky cannon ball had sealed the ILL WIND's fate.
In seconds, pirates swarmed aboard, all chanting words of hate,
"Fight on, lads!" shrieked Cadaverous. "Fight on! You're doing great!"

"You shut it!" said the pirate chief, whose name was Hardboiled Hank.
He was built like a gorilla, and to tell the truth, he stank.
"Ye won't be quite so lippy when I makes ye walk the plank.
But first I'll 'ave yer wallet, see. I 'ope ye caught the bank."

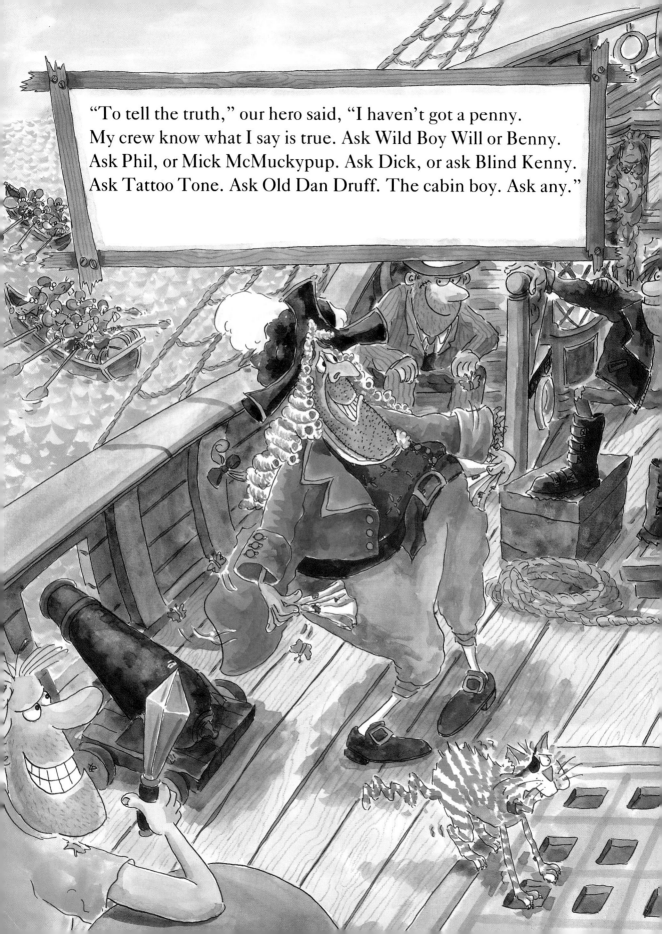

"To tell the truth," our hero said, "I haven't got a penny.
My crew know what I say is true. Ask Wild Boy Will or Benny.
Ask Phil, or Mick McMuckypup. Ask Dick, or ask Blind Kenny.
Ask Tattoo Tone. Ask Old Dan Druff. The cabin boy. Ask any."

"He's lying," Dick Delinquent said. "He's always saying that.
He keeps a bag of precious jewels right underneath 'is 'at.
It ain't my fault I washed the sails. What I say's tit fer tat."
"Thanks very much, Delinquent," said Cadaverous. "You rat."

"Ahar! You'm right!" howled Hardboiled Hank, "I's found 'is little 'oard!"
Into his paws the diamonds and the pearls and rubies poured,
"And now that I got what I wants, you'll walk that plank!" he roared,
"We'll do it after supper, when us pirates gets most bored."

"Oh, do your worst!" the Captain cried, "for I don't give a fig!"
But twenty minutes later, when upon the pirate brig
Clad only in his underpants and vest and powdered wig,
He kicked himself a lot for showing off and talking big.

For all around the pirates stood (though some were sat on kegs)
They passed around a jug of rum and drained it to the dregs.
They pelted him with jellied eels and stale bread rolls and eggs
While pointing at his underpants and laughing at his legs.

You know who else was standing round? His own disloyal crew.
They'd gone and joined the pirates. I don't blame them much, do you?
"Who'll die with me in honour?" cried the Captain. "Tell me, who?"
The seamen gaily chorused, "Are you kidding? Toodleoo."

"Right! That'll do!" bawled Hardboiled Hank. "The sea be nice and rough,
So off ye go, Cadaverous. Let's see ye do yer stuff.
Yer legs *were* entertainin', but with legs, enough's enough.
Let's play another game now. Anyone fer Blind Man's Buff?"

But at these words, a mighty wind comes sweeping from the West,
A wind so strong it tears the hairs from Hank's impressive chest,
It nearly killed Cadaverous, who clutched his skimpy vest
And wished again (alas, in vain) that he was warmly dressed.

"There's rocks ahead! What shall us do? Oh, tell us, Hardboiled Hank!"
But Hank just stares. He's lost his hairs. His mind is now a blank.
The ship, the crew, and Hank (him too) – in seconds, all just sank
Except for poor Cadaverous. You see, HE HAD THE PLANK!!!

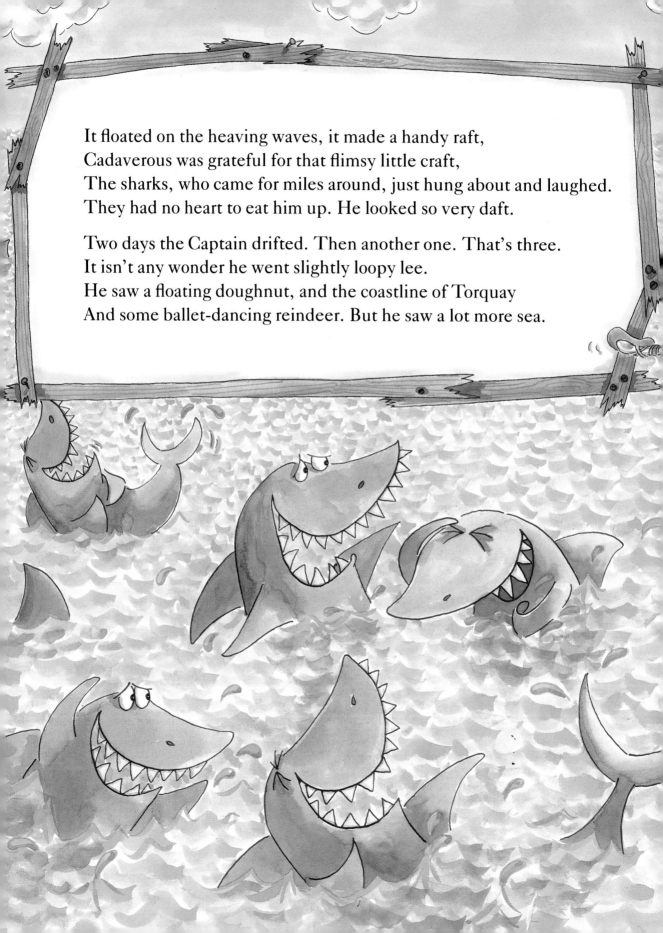

It floated on the heaving waves, it made a handy raft,
Cadaverous was grateful for that flimsy little craft,
The sharks, who came for miles around, just hung about and laughed.
They had no heart to eat him up. He looked so very daft.

Two days the Captain drifted. Then another one. That's three.
It isn't any wonder he went slightly loopy lee.
He saw a floating doughnut, and the coastline of Torquay
And some ballet-dancing reindeer. But he saw a lot more sea.

TORQUAY

He was washed up on an island, and they found him just in time.
They were very kind, those islanders. They brought him drinks of lime
And coconuts and Peewee fish, which tasted quite sublime.
He couldn't speak Baloopisnoot, but managed well with mime.

They nursed him 'til he felt quite well. They fed him juicy fruits,
And using vines and fishing lines, they wove him tailored suits.
"It's here I'll stay," the Captain cried, "it's time I put down roots.
I'll settle on this island with the kind Baloopisnoots."

Captain Cadaverous lay underneath a tree
Feeling calm, content and happy. Yes, as happy as can be.
Then something fell from overhead and plopped into his tea
And that passing cheeky seagull shouted, "Hi! Remember me?"

From that very moment onward, it was downhill all the way.
A whole new set of troubles plunged his life in disarray.
You see, what happened next, to poor Cadaverous' dismay . . .
No. That's another story for another rainy day.